I is for Illusion . . .

Stacks of green bills were piled one on top of another. Everywhere Dink looked, he saw wads and wads of money.

Ruth Rose peeked inside a box. "More money," she said.

"There must be millions of dollars in here!" Josh said. He closed his eyes. "I think I'm gonna throw up."

Suddenly, Dink looked back over his shoulder. "Shhh! I think I heard something!"

A muffled squeaking sound came through the fog. Then there was silence, then another squeak.

Dink gulped, frozen to the spot. "It's coming closer!"

This one is for Tyler Benedict.
—R.R.

To Josh and Jordan
—J.S.G.

Text copyright © 1999 by Ron Roy
Cover art copyright © 2015 by Stephen Gilpin
Interior illustrations copyright © 1999 by John Steven Gurney

All rights reserved. Published in the United States by Random House Children's Books, a division of Random House LLC, a Penguin Random House Company, New York. Originally published in paperback by Random House Children's Books, New York, in 1999.

Random House and the colophon and A to Z Mysteries are registered trademarks and A Stepping Stone Book and the colophon and the A to Z Mysteries colophon are trademarks of Random House LLC.

Visit us on the Web!
SteppingStonesBooks.com
randomhousekids.com

Educators and librarians, for a variety of teaching tools, visit us at RHTeachersLibrarians.com

Library of Congress Cataloging-in-Publication Data
Roy, Ron.
The invisible island / by Ron Roy ; illustrated by John Steven Gurney.
p. cm. — (A to Z mysteries)
"A Stepping Stone book."
Summary: While picnicking on Squall Island, Dink, Josh, and Ruth Rose find a hundred-dollar bill, and when they return to explore further they find an entire cave full of money.
ISBN 978-0-679-89457-5 (trade) — ISBN 978-0-679-99457-2 (lib. bdg.) —
ISBN 978-0-307-53293-0 (ebook)
[1. Islands—Fiction. 2. Counterfeits and counterfeiting—Fiction. 3. Mystery and detective stories.]
I. Gurney, John, ill. II. Title. III. Series: Roy, Ron. A to Z mysteries.
PZ7.R8139In 1999 [Fic]—dc21 99-18346

Printed in the United States of America
46 45

This book has been officially leveled by using the F&P Text Level Gradient™ Leveling System.

Random House Children's Books supports the First Amendment and celebrates the right to read.

A TO Z MYSTERIES®

The Invisible Island

by Ron Roy

illustrated by
John Steven Gurney

A STEPPING STONE BOOK™

Random House 🏠 New York

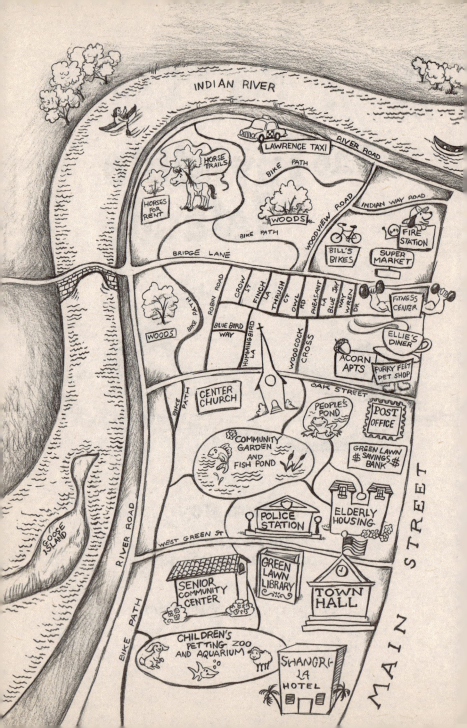

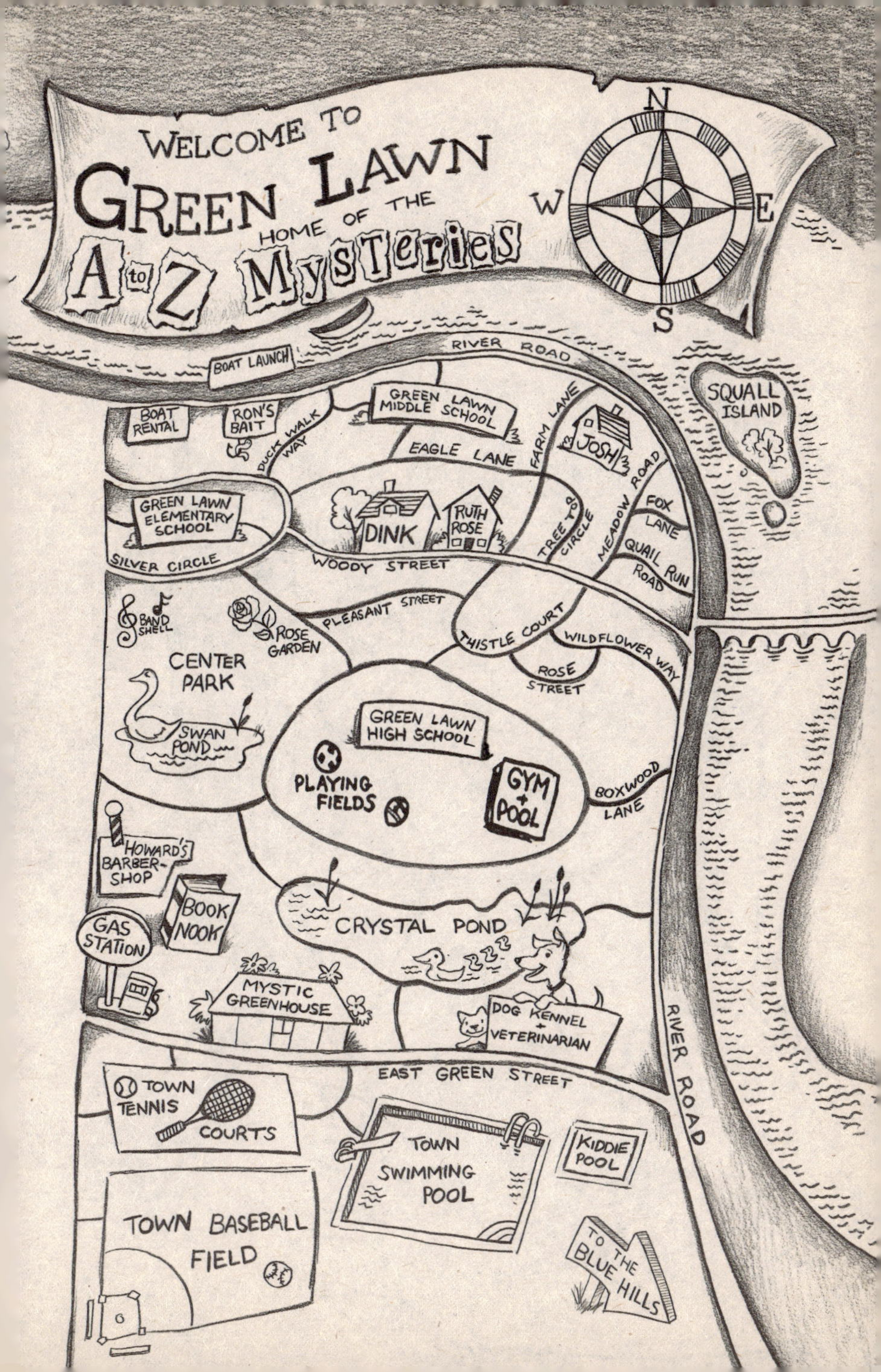
WELCOME TO
GREEN LAWN
HOME OF THE
A to Z Mysteries
N
W
E
S
BOAT LAUNCH
RIVER ROAD
SQUALL ISLAND
BOAT RENTAL
RON'S BAIT
DUCK WALK WAY
GREEN LAWN MIDDLE SCHOOL
EAGLE LANE
FARM LANE
JOSH
MEADOW ROAD
GREEN LAWN ELEMENTARY SCHOOL
DINK
RUTH ROSE
TREE TOP CIRCLE
FOX LANE
QUAIL RUN ROAD
SILVER CIRCLE
WOODY STREET
BAND SHELL
ROSE GARDEN
PLEASANT STREET
THISTLE COURT
WILDFLOWER WAY
ROSE STREET
CENTER PARK
SWAN POND
GREEN LAWN HIGH SCHOOL
PLAYING FIELDS
GYM + POOL
BOXWOOD LANE
HOWARD'S BARBER-SHOP
BOOK NOOK
GAS STATION
CRYSTAL POND
MYSTIC GREENHOUSE
DOG KENNEL + VETERINARIAN
RIVER ROAD
EAST GREEN STREET
TOWN TENNIS COURTS
TOWN SWIMMING POOL
KIDDIE POOL
TOWN BASEBALL FIELD
TO THE BLUE HILLS

Chapter 1

Donald David Duncan, known as Dink to his friends, answered the telephone.

"Duncan residence, Dink speaking."

"Get over here!" Josh Pinto yelled.

Dink jerked the phone away from his ear. "Why?" he asked.

"My mom says we can have a picnic on Squall Island," Josh said. "She made us lunch!"

It was a steaming hot July day.

Splashing around in the Indian River would feel great, thought Dink.

"Okay, let me tell my mom and pick up Ruth Rose. We'll be right over."

Dink ran up the stairs to his parents' room. His mother was sitting at her sewing machine, mending a pair of Dink's jeans.

"Hey, Mom? Me and Josh and Ruth Rose are going to the river for a picnic, okay?" Dink asked.

"Okay, but you kids stay together," she said.

"Thanks, Mom!" Dink pulled on old shorts and his grubbiest sneakers. Before he left, he fed Loretta, his guinea pig. Dink heard her squeak happily as he ran back down the stairs.

Dink hurried over to Ruth Rose's house. Ruth Rose's cat, Tiger, was nursing her kittens on the front step. Dink carefully stepped around them, then rang the bell.

The door opened. Ruth Rose's little brother, Nate, stood in the doorway. He had a cookie in each hand and another in his mouth.

"Hi, Natie," Dink said. "Is your sister here?"

"Shu goofen muppy," Nate said through his cookie.

Dink blinked at Nate. "Huh?"

Ruth Rose appeared next to Nate. "Hi, Dink, what's going on?" she said.

Ruth Rose Hathaway liked to dress all in one color. Today she wore blue shorts, a blue T-shirt, and blue sneakers. Her springy black curls were held in place by a blue headband.

"Josh wants to go to Squall Island for a picnic," Dink said.

Ruth Rose grinned. "Great!" She leaned back into the house. "SEE YOU LATER, MOM! I'M GOING ON A PICNIC WITH THE GUYS!"

Then she bent down and wiped

cookie crumbs from her brother's lips. "Natie, go stay with Mommy, okay? I'll bring you back a magic stone!"

Nate grinned and ran back into the house.

Ruth Rose pulled the door shut. Then she and Dink cut through her backyard and crossed Eagle Lane. A few minutes later, they were at Josh's house.

Josh was in his front yard, holding a garden hose. His little twin brothers, Brian and Bradley, were screaming and racing through the water.

"Hi," Josh said when he saw Dink and Ruth Rose. He shut off the water.

"Gotta go," he told Brian and Bradley. "Be good boys and don't leave the yard!"

Josh grabbed his backpack off the porch. "Hope you guys're hungry," he said. "Mom packed a lot of food."

"That should last you about three minutes!" Dink said, grinning.

The kids hiked through the field behind Josh's house. Then they crossed River Road and walked to the bank of the Indian River.

The river flowed slowly, rippling over a few large rocks. In most places, the water was shallow enough to wade across. Trees and shrubbery grew along the banks. Birds and squirrels chattered in the greenery.

The kids walked along the river, slapping at mosquitoes. They stopped when they saw Squall Island.

The small island sat in the middle of the river. It was mostly sand, shrubs, and rocks. No trees grew there, and no animals made the island their home. But the kids loved the sandy beach and clean, shallow water.

They waded in, wearing their

sneakers. Soon they were up to their knees.

"Boy, this feels good!" Dink said as the cool water climbed his sweaty legs. He kicked water at Josh and Ruth Rose. They splashed him back, and pretty soon all three were soaked.

A few minutes later, they flopped down on the island's small beach. Dink took off his sneakers and wiggled his toes in the warm sand.

"Let's eat!" Josh said. He opened his backpack and brought out plastic bags holding sandwiches, slices of watermelon, and cookies.

"I wonder what it would be like to be stranded on an island," he said.

Dink chewed his sandwich. "Josh, we couldn't get stranded out here. All we'd have to do is wade back to shore."

Josh had a faraway look in his eyes. "Yeah, but what if pirates buried treasure here?" he said. He dug a hole in the sand with his heel. "We could be sitting over a chest filled with gold!"

"I don't think there were any pirates in Connecticut," Ruth Rose pointed out.

"Why not?" Josh asked. He gestured toward the vine-covered boulders in the center of the island. "This would be a perfect place for a pirate hideout!"

"Ahoy, mate!" Dink said.

Ruth Rose stood up. "I want to explore," she said. She walked toward the water. "I promised Nate I'd bring him a magic stone."

"What's a magic stone?" Dink asked. He followed her to the water's edge.

"This is!" Ruth Rose held up a smooth, pure white pebble.

"What makes it magic?"

"Nate has a bunch of these in his room," Ruth Rose said. "My parents told him if he kept his room neat, the stones would turn into nickels."

Josh joined Dink and Ruth Rose. He

handed each of them a cookie. "And Nate believed them?"

Ruth Rose grinned. "When Nate cleans his room, Mom sneaks in and takes one of the stones! She leaves a nickel in its place."

The kids started walking along the shore. The sun felt hot on Dink's back, so he took off his shirt.

"Hey, guys, look!" Josh yelled. He was standing over a footprint. "Somebody else has been here!"

He grinned at Dink and Ruth Rose. "Maybe it was Blackbeard!"

Dink stepped into the footprint. It was twice as big as his foot!

"I don't know about Blackbeard," he said, "but whoever this was has *really* big feet!"

"Look, here's another one!" Ruth Rose said. "And another!"

The kids followed the footprints

away from the water. They led toward the boulders at the center of the island.

The footprints stopped suddenly in front of a squat, vine-covered boulder.

"That's funny," Dink said. "What'd the guy do, jump over these rocks?"

"Maybe he walked around them," Josh said.

Dink and Josh began to circle the boulders slowly, looking for more footprints.

Ruth Rose started walking in the other direction. Suddenly, Dink heard her yell, "HEY, GUYS! COME OVER HERE QUICK!"

Dink and Josh ran back the way they'd come.

"Look!" Ruth Rose said, pointing down between her feet. Something green was poking out of the sand.

"What is it?" Josh asked.

"MONEY!" Ruth Rose yelled.

Chapter 2

"A ten-dollar bill!" Josh said, grabbing the bill and holding it up.

"Wrong," Dink said, plucking it out of Josh's fingers. "Count the zeroes!"

Josh's mouth fell open.

Ruth Rose's blue eyes got huge.

Dink was holding a hundred-dollar bill!

"A hundred bucks!" Josh squeaked.

He reached for the bill, but Dink quickly handed the money to Ruth Rose.

"She found it," he said.

"But who lost it?" Ruth Rose asked, shoving the bill into a pocket.

Dink pointed to the footprints in the sand. "Maybe he did."

The kids stared at the footprints.

"Maybe he lost more," Josh said. "Let's search!"

The kids separated. With their eyes on the ground, they climbed over boulders and peeked under bushes. They found plenty of poison ivy, but no more hundred-dollar bills.

"Hey, guys, look at this," Dink called from near the water's edge.

Josh and Ruth Rose ran to where he was standing.

Dink pointed to a long patch of sand that was perfectly smooth. It looked as if someone had scraped a board over the sand, flattening all the little bumps.

"I'll bet somebody came out here with a rowboat," Ruth Rose said. "This must be where they dragged it up on the beach."

"I wonder if the same person who brought the boat made those footprints," Dink said, pulling his T-shirt back on.

"And dropped that hundred-dollar bill," said Josh.

Ruth Rose patted her pocket. "I don't know, but we have to try to find him."

"Why?" Josh said, grinning. "Think of what we could buy with that money. Split three ways, of course!"

"Forget it, Josh," Ruth Rose said. "The money isn't ours. We have to return it."

"To who?"

"To whoever lost it," Dink said.

"And how are we supposed to find the guy?" Josh asked.

The kids sat in the sand and thought.

"I know," Ruth Rose said. "We can go to Ron's Bait Shop. Maybe Mr. P knows who was out here."

"Good idea," Dink said.

"Boy," said Josh, getting to his feet. "You guys sure wanna get rid of that money fast."

"How would *you* feel if you lost a hundred-dollar bill?" Ruth Rose asked Josh.

He grinned. "Trust me, if I ever got one, I'd *never* lose it! Anyway, let's eat the watermelon my mom packed. Those cookies made my mouth dry."

They walked back to Josh's pack and slurped on sweet, juicy chunks of watermelon. They spit the seeds at each other as they packed up.

Josh shrugged into his backpack. "Well, if we have to return the money, maybe we'll get our names in the paper," he said. He scratched his ankles. "Maybe we'll get a reward!"

Ruth Rose giggled. "Josh, the only thing you're going to get is poison ivy!"

Chapter 3

The kids waded back into the river. A few minutes later, they were squishing their way up River Road to Ron's Bait Shop.

Ron Pinkowski lived in an old house next to the river. On the ground floor, he sold bait, boating supplies, and groceries. He also repaired and painted boats and fixed boat motors.

The kids trudged down a dusty driveway to the house. Several small

boats were lined up in Mr. Pinkowski's
big yard along the riverbank. A striped
cat slept on the back step. Out the back
door trailed a long orange extension
cord. The kids followed the cord around
the side of the house.

They spotted Mr. Pinkowski under a
shady tree, sanding a boat bottom.

"Hi, Mr. P," Dink said.

Ron Pinkowski switched off the electric sander. He was tall and sandy-haired, and sported a curly beard and droopy mustache.

"Well, hi, kids. What're you up to today?" he asked, smiling.

Ruth Rose pulled the hundred-dollar bill out of her pocket. "I just found this on Squall Island," she said.

"Goodness," Ron said. "Aren't you a lucky gal!"

"We saw some marks in the sand from a boat," Dink said.

"And some footprints, too," Josh added. "Really big ones!"

"We think whoever was out there might have lost the money," Ruth Rose said.

"Hmm, wonder who it coulda been." Ron leaned against the boat and tugged on his beard. "Not many folks go out there.

The poison ivy grows somethin' fierce in all that sand."

"Yeah, and I think I walked right through some!" Josh said, scratching his leg.

Ron smiled. "All I have to do is *look* at the stuff and I swell up like a balloon," he said.

"Could we leave a note here about the money?" Ruth Rose asked.

"Good idea, Ruth Rose. I'll stick it up near my bait tanks."

The kids followed Ron into his bait shop, where he handed Ruth Rose a pencil and pad.

She thought for a minute, then wrote:

If you lost money on Squall Island, call 555-9916.

"Shouldn't you say how much you found?" Josh asked.

Ruth Rose shook her head. "If I write the amount, anyone could call and claim it, even if they didn't lose it."

Ron tacked Ruth Rose's note to a small bulletin board. "Lots of people will see it here," he said.

"Thanks, Mr. P," Ruth Rose said. "I hope whoever lost the money sees the note."

Ron grinned. "Wish it was me!"

The kids laughed. They said good-bye and headed for Duck Walk Way.

"So what're you gonna do with the money?" Josh asked Ruth Rose. "I'll be glad to hold on to it for you!"

Ruth Rose shook her head. "Nope. I'm giving it to Officer Fallon. It'll be safe at the police station."

Josh scratched his arm. "Let's stop at Ellie's on the way. Maybe an ice cream cone will help me forget about this lousy poison ivy!"

The kids crossed the elementary school's wide lawn and hiked down Main Street. As they opened the door to Ellie's Diner, cool air washed over them.

After they ordered cones, Ruth Rose asked Ellie if she knew anyone who had lost money on Squall Island.

"Someone with really huge feet!" Dink added.

Ellie shook her head. "Hon, I don't even know anyone who goes out there. I hear it's covered with poison ivy!"

She noticed Josh scratching. "Looks like someone else is covered with the stuff!"

The kids thanked Ellie and left. They worked on their cones on the way to the police station.

"I can't believe we're gonna just

give away a hundred bucks," Josh said.

"If I get a reward," Ruth Rose said, "I'll split it with you guys."

Josh grinned. "Now you're talking!"

They found Officer Fallon sitting at his desk. He was watching his computer screen and sipping a glass of lemonade.

"Howdy," he said as the kids trooped in. "What can I do for you?"

"Look at this!" Ruth Rose said. She placed the hundred-dollar bill on his desk.

Officer Fallon picked up the bill and examined it. "Where'd this come from?" he asked.

"Ruth Rose found it on Squall Island," Josh told him. "We were out there having a picnic, and it was in the sand!"

"I'm trying to find out who lost it," Ruth Rose said. "Mr. Pinkowski let me put a note on his bulletin board. I left my phone number."

"This bill could've been lost a long

time ago," Officer Fallon said. "Not many folks go to Squall Island."

He grinned at Ruth Rose. "If no one claims it, the money is yours to keep."

"Really?" Ruth Rose said. "Cool!"

Officer Fallon put the bill in an envelope and sealed it. He wrote the date and Ruth Rose's name on the outside.

"I'll put this in our safe," he said. "If it's still here in thirty days, I'll let you know."

The kids thanked Officer Fallon and left.

"Gee, Ruth Rose," Josh said as they waited for the light on Main Street. "Will you split the hundred three ways if you get to keep it?"

"I might," she said. "If you're extra nice to me!"

"I'm always nice to you!"

Dink whispered something in Ruth Rose's ear.

"Okay, prove you're nice," she told Josh. "Come over tomorrow and mow my lawn!"

Josh laughed. "I have a better idea. Let's go back to the island and look for more money!"

"Josh, we already did, and there wasn't any," Dink said.

"But we never found where the footprints ended," Josh argued. "I'll bet if we do, we'll find buried treasure!"

"What about the poison ivy?" Ruth Rose reminded him.

Josh scratched his neck. "So what's a little poison ivy?" he said. "I'm going back to Squall Island tomorrow, and I'm bringing a shovel!"

He grinned at his friends. "You coming with me? Or do I keep the treasure all to myself?"

Chapter 4

Dink yawned and looked out the kitchen window the next morning.

"Fog," he muttered. He finished his cereal and put the bowl in the sink.

Just then, the doorbell rang. It was Josh, standing on the porch holding a shovel. "You ready to go?" he asked.

"It's so foggy," Dink said, looking over Josh's shoulders. "I can hardly see across the street! We won't find the island, let alone a treasure."

"If there's more money out there, I'll find it," Josh said, scratching his ankle. "Let's get Ruth Rose."

"I'm already here!" Ruth Rose said, appearing out of the fog.

When she saw Josh scratching, she said, "You better put something on that poison ivy, Joshua!"

"My mom said the same thing," Josh said. He scratched his arm. "She gave me money to buy some calamine lotion. Now let's get going!"

Balancing the shovel over one shoulder, Josh led his friends through Ruth Rose's backyard and across Meadow Road. The tall, dewy grass on the other side soaked their sneakers and legs.

Near the river, the fog was even thicker. It hung in tree branches like miniature clouds. The kids' faces and hair were wet.

"I can't even see the river," Dink muttered.

"It's right here," Josh said, splashing the water with his shovel.

"Yeah, but where's the island?" Ruth Rose asked.

The kids gazed out to where they thought Squall Island should be. All they could see was more fog. One patch looked a little darker than the rest.

"That must be it," Josh said, stepping into the water. "Come on, guys, I can almost smell the money!"

"Like a hound dog," Dink muttered.

The river was quiet. No birds sang. The kids' legs splashing through the water made the only sound.

Dink began to imagine some fog monster creeping toward him. It had slimy green tentacles and six-inch-long teeth!

Dink was glad when the water

became shallower. Suddenly, his foot struck dry land. They were on Squall Island again!

The kids stopped and looked around. Wisps of fog hung over everything. Dink could barely make out the mound of boulders in the center of the island. He remembered yesterday's sun on his back and shivered.

"This place is creepy in the fog," Ruth Rose said. "I hope the sun comes out soon!"

"Okay, Joshua," Dink said. "You got us out here. Now what?"

Josh dropped to his hands and knees. "Help me find the big footprints again," he said.

The kids quickly found the prints and followed them to the squat, vine-covered boulder.

"So where'd Bigfoot go from here?" Josh muttered.

"It looks like the guy walked right into this big rock," Dink said.

"Maybe he climbed over it," Ruth Rose said.

Josh poked his shovel into the poison ivy vines covering the boulder. The shovel clinked against stone. Josh tried another spot. This time the shovel went straight in.

"Hey, guys!" Josh said. "I think I found something!"

Using the shovel to keep the vines back, Josh peered into a dark space.

"There're two boulders here!" he said.

"And look," Ruth Rose said. "A little path goes right between them!"

The path was hidden, covered with poison ivy leaves and vines.

"He must have gone through there," Dink said.

"But it's all poison ivy!" Ruth Rose said.

"Wait a sec," Josh said. He chopped

at the poison ivy with his shovel until he had cleared a passage. "Just be careful," he said.

Single file, the kids walked down the narrow path. Enormous boulders loomed over them on each side.

Soon they came to a small, sandy clearing in the middle of the rocks. The rocks were thick with poison ivy. The dew-covered leaves were dull green in the fog.

"I feel like I'm in some jungle!" Ruth Rose said.

"More prints!" Josh said, dropping down on his knees.

Dink got down next to Josh. "They look like they're from the same guy," Dink said. "But there are so many! And they walk all over each other."

"Now what, Josh?" Ruth Rose asked.

"Now we search for treasure," Josh said. "We'll take turns and dig all over this place!"

They began digging hole after hole. Ruth Rose found a rusty nail, but no treasure.

Soon the kids were sweaty and covered with sand. Josh started filling the holes back in so no one would step in them.

Dink flopped down against one of the boulders.

"WATCH OUT!" Ruth Rose yelled.

Dink jumped away from the rock.

Something was sticking him through his shirt!

"Ouch! What's poking me?" he asked. He turned around so Josh and Ruth Rose could see his back. "Can you see anything?"

Josh grinned. "Just a hunk of poison ivy," he said.

"Stop grinning and get it off me!" Dink yelled.

"I'll get it," Ruth Rose said. She

brushed at the twig with the shovel handle.

"Is it gone?" Dink asked, trying to see over his shoulder.

"This is amazing!" Ruth Rose said. "Look, Josh!"

"I don't believe it," Josh said.

"What's amazing?" Dink cried. "What're you guys *doing* back there?" He was already feeling itchy.

"This poison ivy is fake!" Ruth Rose said.

"Huh?" Dink turned around. Ruth Rose handed him a green sprig. The leaves were plastic and the stem was made of brown wire.

"I don't get it," Dink said. "Why would anyone . . ."

"This is too weird," Josh said. He placed the shovel blade between the boulder and the fake poison ivy. Then he twisted the shovel and pried off a section of vines. It came away from the face of the boulder in a sheet and fell flat on the ground.

"The whole rock is covered with plastic poison ivy," Ruth Rose said. "Tied to a wooden frame!"

"Forget that," Josh said. "Look what was under this stuff!"

The "boulder" wasn't a boulder at all. The kids were staring at a large square cement slab.

Chapter 5

"What is it?" Dink and Ruth Rose asked at the same time.

"It looks like a cement refrigerator!" Josh said.

Ruth Rose laughed. "Gee, Josh, I wonder if there's food in it!"

"Very funny!" Josh climbed up on some smaller rocks and hoisted himself to the top of the slab.

"It's flat up here, too," he said. "This thing is a big cement box!"

"Is this front part a door?" Ruth Rose asked. She poked the flat slab with the shovel.

Dink ran his fingers along the sides. "I can't find any hinges," he said. He tugged at it, but it didn't budge.

"Maybe there's a secret lock somewhere," Ruth Rose suggested. She began digging around the bottom of the slab. All she found was stones and poison ivy roots.

"Ouch!" Josh said, still on top. "There's something sharp up here!"

He poked his head over the top. "Climb up here, guys. I think I found the key to this thing!"

Dink and Ruth Rose scrambled up next to Josh.

"Look at this," Josh said. He pointed to a metal rod poking out of the cement.

"Try pulling on it," Dink suggested.

Josh grabbed the rod and yanked.

"Doesn't come out," he muttered.

"Does it wiggle back and forth?" Ruth Rose asked.

She put her foot against the rod and shoved. It still didn't budge.

"Well, it has to do *something*," Dink said.

He climbed down off the cement box, grabbed the shovel, and handed it up to Josh.

"Try hitting it with that," he said.

Josh held the shovel over his head, braced himself, and gave the rod a good smack.

Suddenly, they heard a scratchy noise, like fingernails on a chalkboard.

"Whoa, that did it!" Dink yelled, jumping back. "It's moving!"

The cement door swung open, revealing a damp, musty closet.

Dink took a step forward, then stopped. His jaw dropped.

"What's in there?" Josh asked, staring down at Dink.

Dink didn't answer.

"Dink?" Ruth Rose said. "What's going on?"

Dink gulped and tried to speak. "Muh-muh-muh . . ."

"What the heck is 'muh'?" Josh said. "Mud? Mummies? Muffins?"

Dink could barely breathe, let alone talk.

"Money!" he finally said.

Chapter 6

Josh and Ruth Rose scrambled down and stared into the opening.

Inside, it was like a vault. Metal shelves had been attached to the cement walls with thick bolts. And every shelf held money.

Stacks of green bills were piled one on top of another. Everywhere Dink looked, he saw wads and wads of money.

"There must be millions of dollars

in here!" Josh said. He closed his eyes. "I think I'm gonna throw up."

"But whose money is it?" Ruth Rose asked. "Who put it here?"

Dink stepped inside the vault. On the bottom shelves were cardboard boxes with HAPPY HEART DOG FOOD written on the sides.

"Dog food?" he said.

Josh and Ruth Rose crowded into the vault. Ruth Rose peeked into two of the boxes.

"More money," she said.

Suddenly, Dink looked back over his shoulder. "Shhh!" he whispered. "I think I heard something!"

The kids stood perfectly still and listened.

"There it is again!" Dink said.

A muffled squeaking sound came through the fog. Then there was silence, then another squeak.

Dink gulped, frozen to the spot. "It's coming closer!" he whispered.

"M-maybe it's the p-pirate!" Josh said.

"It could be the guy with big feet!" said Ruth Rose. "Maybe this is *his* treasure!"

"Let's get out of here!" Dink said.

"Help me close this thing!"

The kids swung the cement door shut. Josh grabbed his shovel while Dink and Ruth Rose lifted the plastic poison ivy back into place. Now the cement safe was hidden again.

Dink quickly led the way back through the boulders to the water.

On the narrow beach, they stood in the fog and listened.

Dink heard the squeaking sound again, then a soft thud, then silence.

Slowly, a small boat drifted out of the fog. A large, dark figure sat hunched in the stern. Dink didn't dare move or say anything. It looked as if the figure was staring at them!

After what seemed like a year, the figure began to row away. Dink heard the oars squeak as the boat vanished back into the fog.

"Wh-who was that?" Josh croaked.

"I don't know," Dink said.

"Whoever it was, let's get off this island!" Ruth Rose said.

The kids quietly stepped into the shallow water. Trying not to splash, they waded to shore. Dink kept watch for the boat and its silent passenger. But he couldn't see anything through the fog.

Behind them, Squall Island became invisible once more.

Ten minutes later, they flung open the door to Officer Fallon's office.

Officer Fallon looked up from his computer. "What's wrong, kids? You look like you've seen a ghost!"

He stared at their soggy sneakers. "And you're all wet!"

"We found more money," Ruth Rose said. "Millions of dollars!"

Officer Fallon raised one eyebrow.

"Really, we did!" Josh said.

"Okay, sit down and talk to me," Officer Fallon said, switching off his computer.

The kids perched on the edges of their chairs.

"We went back to the island," Dink explained, "and found a cement safe. It had stacks of money in it!"

They told Officer Fallon about the secret path, the plastic poison ivy, and the hidden cement vault.

"Just before we left, we saw some-one in a rowboat," Josh said. "I think he was coming to the island, but then he turned around and left!"

Officer Fallon sat up. "Did you get a good look at him?" he asked.

"It was too foggy," Dink said.

Officer Fallon frowned and nodded.

"Why would anyone keep money on Squall Island?" Ruth Rose asked. "Why wouldn't they just keep it in a regular bank?"

Officer Fallon looked at Ruth Rose. "Because it's not real money," he said.

"It's *not*?" Ruth Rose asked. "What is it, then?"

"I guess there's no reason not to tell you," Officer Fallon said. "After you left yesterday, I remembered something I read a few weeks ago about counterfeit money. I took a closer look at the bill you found."

He pulled the envelope from his drawer and removed the hundred-dollar bill. "This is counterfeit, kids. And I'm guessing the money in your cement safe is counterfeit, too."

"Counterfeit?" Josh gasped. "You mean it's all fake?"

Officer Fallon smiled. "Sorry, Josh."

"But who put it there?" Dink asked.

"That's what we're trying to find out," Officer Fallon said.

He stood and walked the kids to the door. "Officer Keene and I will go out there for a look today. Starting now, we'll be keeping an eye on that island."

Officer Fallon opened his office door. "Off you go now. And promise me you'll stay away from that island. Counterfeiters can be dangerous!"

The kids thanked Officer Fallon and left. As they walked up Main Street, Dink thought about the mysterious figure he'd seen in the boat. Was it the counterfeiter? Had he seen the three of them standing on the beach?

Dink swallowed. Were he and Josh and Ruth Rose in danger?

Chapter 7

Josh scratched his knee, then his neck, then his left elbow.

"Guess I'd better buy some cala- mine lotion," he said.

"We're almost at the supermarket," Dink said. He glanced over his shoulder.

"What're you looking at?" Ruth Rose asked.

Dink shrugged. "Nothing, I guess. I just keep thinking about that creepy guy in the boat."

"Do you think he recognized us?" Josh asked. "I mean, if we couldn't see his face, maybe he couldn't see ours."

"I hope you're right," Dink said. "If the guy in the boat *was* the counterfeiter, he could be anyone, even someone we know!"

"Oh, great, Dinkus," Josh said. "Now I'm going to have nightmares!"

The kids walked into the supermarket and headed for the pharmacy. Mrs. Hernandez looked up and smiled.

"Hi, kids, what do you need?" she asked.

Josh scratched his knee. "Do you have any calamine lotion?" he asked.

Mrs. Hernandez came out from behind her counter. She gave Josh a once-over.

"That's poison ivy, all right," she said. She took a pink bottle from a shelf and handed it to Josh. "That's my last bottle. Ron Pinkowski came in yesterday and bought up my other three."

Josh paid Mrs. Hernandez and thanked her. Then the kids left the

store. They sat on a bench while Josh dabbed calamine lotion on his itchy spots.

"I wonder why Mr. P needs this stuff," Ruth Rose said. "Didn't he tell us he stays away from poison ivy?"

"He wasn't scratching when we saw him yesterday," Dink said.

Suddenly, Josh jumped to his feet. "Oh, my gosh! It's him!"

Dink looked around. "Who's him?"

"Mr. Pinkowski!" Josh said. "He bought the calamine lotion because he's got poison ivy. And he's got poison ivy because he was on Squall Island hiding his counterfeit money!"

Dink shook his head. "If Mr. P has poison ivy, he could've gotten it anywhere."

"Maybe he's hiding a printing press in one of his empty fish tanks!" Josh said.

"Josh, what are you talking about?" Ruth Rose asked.

"It's perfect!" Josh said. "He sells bait to fool people, but he's really getting rich making phony money!"

"That's crazy," Dink said. "Just because Mr. P bought calamine lotion doesn't mean he's a counterfeiter."

Josh screwed the bottle cap on and shoved the lotion into a pocket. "I'm not crazy!" he said. "He's tall, so he's probably got big feet, right?"

Ruth Rose opened her mouth, but Josh cut her off.

"And he lives right on the river," Josh went on. "He's got boats! He knows Squall Island is the perfect place to stash money. It *has* to be him!"

Dink looked at Ruth Rose. "What do you think?" he asked her.

"It could have been Mr. Pinkowski in the boat," Ruth Rose said. "But he's

our friend. I can't believe he's a counterfeiter!"

"I can't either," Dink said.

"Well, I can!" Josh said. He scratched
his stomach. "Let's go back to the bait
shop and see if he has poison ivy."

"But how will we know?" Ruth Rose
asked.

Josh grinned. "He bought three bottles of calamine lotion," he reminded
her. "He'll be pink!"

Dink laughed. "Okay, let's go back
to the bait shop," he said. "You look for
poison ivy. I want to see if Mr. P's feet
are as big as those footprints!"

Chapter 8

"Well, you were right about one thing,"
Ruth Rose whispered to Josh. "Mr.
Pinkowski *does* have big feet!"

"Yeah, but they still don't look as
big as those footprints we saw," Dink
whispered back.

The kids were hiding behind the
bushes near Ron's Bait Shop. Ron was
standing in his yard, rubbing a cloth
over a small green rowboat.

"Look at that boat!" Josh said. "It

could be the one we saw out at the island!"

"But I don't see any calamine lotion on him," Dink said. "And he's not scratching!"

Just then, a black car pulled into the driveway. Ron waved as a man in a dark suit stepped out of the car.

The man waved back, then leaned into the car and pulled out a box. On its side were written four words: HAPPY HEART DOG FOOD!

Josh gasped. "Do you see . . ."

"Shhh!" whispered Ruth Rose.

The kids watched as the man handed Ron the box. Ron turned and carried it into his shed.

When Ron came out, he handed the box back to the stranger. The man put it on the seat of his car, then took out a checkbook. Quickly, he scribbled out a check and handed it to Ron.

Finally, he climbed back in his car and drove away.

"Check out the license plate!" Ruth Rose said.

Dink read the plate. "B, E, N, T. BENT? What's that mean?" he asked.

"Who cares?" Josh said. "Mr. P just sold that guy a boxful of counterfeit money! Let's go tell Officer Fallon!"

"Josh, that box could have been full of dog food," Dink said.

"Dinkus, think!" Josh said. "Someone hid fake money in those same dog
food boxes on Squall Island. I say one
of those two guys is the counterfeiter!"

"Josh could be right," Ruth Rose
pointed out. "But before we go see
Officer Fallon, maybe we can find out
who that other man is."

"How?" Dink asked.

"Let's ask at the gas station," Ruth
Rose said. "Mr. Holly might know who
drives a black car with BENT on the
license plate."

When the kids reached the gas station,
Mr. Holly was nowhere in sight.

Then Dink heard someone whist-
ling. The tune was coming from under
a banged-up red pickup truck.

"Mr. Holly?" Dink said. "Is that you?"

A round, grease-smudged face popped
out from under the truck.

"Howdy," Mr. Holly said, grinning

at the kids. "You got car trouble?"

"Sort of," Ruth Rose said. "Do you know who owns a car with BENT on the license plate?"

Mr. Holly stood up and wiped his hands on a rag. "Why, is the car bent?" he said, winking at Dink.

Dink laughed. "No, but we need to find the driver," he said.

"I found some money," Ruth Rose said. "We think it might be his."

"Sounds like those new folks," Mr. Holly said, "Mr. and Mrs. Warden Bent. Few weeks ago, they rented a small house on Fox Lane. I put a set of spark plugs in that snazzy Lincoln of theirs."

"Fox Lane!" Dink said, giving Josh a look. "That's over by the river!"

"Right-o," Mr. Holly said. "Nice view of the water. Now if you'll excuse me, this old truck needs my help!"

The kids thanked Mr. Holly and left the gas station.

"We know who the guy is now," Dink said, "but we still can't prove he or Mr. P is a counterfeiter."

"But the box—" Josh started to say.

"We don't know what was in it," Dink reminded him.

"Right," Ruth Rose said. "Why don't we go to Mr. Bent's house and wait for him to come home? Maybe we can get a peek at the box when he goes in his house."

"Okay, but let's be careful," Dink said. "I don't want to end up locked in that vault on Squall Island!"

Chapter 9

The kids crossed Thistle Court and headed toward Fox Lane.

There were only three small houses on the narrow lane. The last one was a cottage nearly hidden in trees and thick bushes. Somewhere, a bird let out a single chirp.

Josh nudged Dink. "The car!" he whispered, pointing.

The same black car was parked under a tree. The license plate said BENT.

The kids snuck up to the car. All three peered through a rear window.

There was no Happy Heart Dog Food box on the car's seats or floor.

"He must've taken it into the house," Dink said, crouching down next to Josh and Ruth Rose.

"Now what do we do?" Josh asked.

"We could try getting inside the house," Ruth Rose said.

Josh looked at her. "How?"

"What if we ring the bell and say we're selling Girl Scout cookies?"

Josh rolled his eyes. "Yeah, right, two boys selling Girl Scout cookies!"

"Okay, then I'll do it alone," Ruth Rose said.

"No way," Dink said. "No one's going into that house. If the Bents are the counterfeiters, they're dangerous!"

"So what do we do?" Josh asked. "I sure could use a sandwich!"

Suddenly, the front door opened. A short-legged hound dog with floppy ears waddled out onto the porch. The dog was brown and white, with big, sad eyes.

"Stay near the house, Shorty," a voice said.

"Uh-oh," Josh whispered.

"Let's get out of here before he smells us!" Ruth Rose said.

The kids melted into the thick shrubbery growing wild on both sides of the cottage. They crept toward the back-yard, trying to be as quiet as possible.

"Look," Dink said, pointing to a small garage at the very back of the property. Except for the door, the garage was surrounded by bushes. "We can hide there!"

Just then, the dog let out a howl.

Ruth Rose looked over her shoulder. "Oh, no! He's after us!"

The kids sprinted behind the garage. Dink found a low window.

"In here!" he said, shoving the window sash up.

The dog came loping around the corner with its nose to the ground.

"Nice doggie," Josh whispered.

The hound looked at Josh and let out another howl.

"Quick, inside!" Dink said. He dove through the open window.

Josh and Ruth Rose piled into the garage on top of Dink. Outside, the dog started barking. Dink saw its black snout and eyes peeking over the sill. He shoved Josh off him and closed the window.

The dog was still barking. It scratched at the window with its big feet.

"We have to hide!" Dink said. "The Bents are bound to hear all that noise!"

The kids quickly looked around.

Against one wall, a workbench was piled with junk. Dink noticed a tarp-covered mound opposite the bench.

Josh and Ruth Rose dove under the bench. Dink headed for the tarp. He lifted one edge, crawled underneath, and let the tarp drop over his back.

It was dark under the tarp. Dink couldn't see a thing. He found himself sprawled on top of several hard boxes with sharp edges.

Suddenly, the dog stopped barking. Dink thought he heard a human voice.

He lifted a corner of the tarp and peeked toward the window. Through the dirty glass, Dink saw a woman's legs. She bent down, picked up the dog, and carried him out of sight.

Barely breathing, Dink waited until he felt sure the woman wasn't coming back. Then he crawled out from under the tarp. On the other side of the garage, Josh and Ruth Rose came out from under the bench.

"That was close!" Ruth Rose said.

Dink looked around. They were standing on a cement floor. The air was cool and dry. In one corner stood gardening tools and a few fishing poles.

Then Dink spotted something. "Look!" he said.

On top of the workbench sat a Happy Heart Dog Food box.

"Maybe it's the one Mr. Bent had in his car!" Dink said. He yanked open the box flaps. Inside, he found only a paint can with green smears on its sides.

Dink thought for a minute. "Guys, remember that boat Mr. P was working on? It was green, right?"

He held up the paint can. "Maybe the boat belongs to Mr. Bent, and Ron painted it for him. This could be the leftover paint."

"Then the check Mr. Bent gave him was to pay for the paint job!" Ruth Rose said.

She reached into the box and pulled out a wadded ball of paper. She flattened it on the workbench.

"It's a receipt from the pharmacy," Ruth Rose said. "For three bottles of calamine lotion!"

Dink stared at the receipt. It was from a credit card. Neatly printed on the bottom of the piece of paper was the name Ronald W. Pinkowski.

"Hey, guys, check this out!"

Josh had been poking around the other side of the garage. Hanging on wall pegs were two pairs of long green wading boots.

Josh unhooked one pair and took it down. "Look at the size of this foot!" he said.

Dink walked over for a closer look.

"*These* must be what made those big footprints!" he said.

Ruth Rose examined the bottom of one of the boots. Wedged into the treads were tiny pebbles and sand.

The kids stared at each other.

"Now what do we do?" Josh asked.

"Now we go tell Officer Fallon what we found," Dink said.

He tiptoed over to the garage door and peeked through a crack.

"Uh-oh," Dink said. "We're in trouble, guys. Mrs. Bent just brought out some food. She's lighting the grill!"

"Great," Josh muttered. "And I'm stuck in here, starving to death!"

He and Ruth Rose joined Dink at the crack.

"Look!" Ruth Rose said.

A tall man walked up to the grill. It was the man they'd seen at Ron's Bait Shop. But now he was wearing shorts and a T-shirt.

His long arms and legs were blotched with calamine lotion.

Chapter 10

Ruth Rose let out a small gasp. "He's the one who got poison ivy on Squall Island! The calamine lotion was for *him*!"

"But Mr. Pinkowski bought it," Josh said. "I still say they're in it together!"

Dink peeked through the garage door crack again. "Mr. Bent's reading a newspaper," he whispered. "Mrs. Bent's cooking hamburgers."

"Is the dog there?" Josh asked.

"Yep."

"If we try to leave, the dog will probably start barking again," Ruth Rose said.

"Those hamburgers smell so good!" Josh said. He let out a little groan.

"Don't think about food," Dink said. "Think about a way to get us out of here!"

"Okay, I will!" Josh said. He shoved Dink aside and put an eye to the crack. "I have a plan," he said after a minute.

"Tell us!" Ruth Rose said.

Josh grinned. "Let's invite the Bents into the garage!"

Ruth Rose shook her head. "The poison ivy has finally gotten to his brain," she said to Dink.

"No, listen," Josh said. "We'll make a lot of noise. The Bents and poochie will hear it. They'll come flying in here to find out what's going on and—"

"And catch us in their garage!" Dink interrupted.

Josh smiled devilishly. "Nope, because we'll be hopping out the window. They'll never see us!"

Dink nodded thoughtfully. "It could work," he said. "But I think we need to figure out a way to keep them in here long enough for us to get away."

"I have an idea!" Ruth Rose walked over to the workbench. "There must be something to write with," she muttered.

"What're you gonna write?" Josh asked.

"Aha!" Ruth Rose pulled a hunk of carpenter's chalk out of a toolbox.

She kneeled on the floor and printed in large letters:

I know about your counterfeit money. Let's talk or I go to the cops. Meet me on Squall Island in an hour.

"Oh, my gosh!" Josh yelped.

"But what if they just go out to the island, take the money, and leave town?" Dink asked.

"Exactly! When they do, Officer Fallon will be waiting for them!" Ruth Rose said.

Josh found a hammer in the tool-box. "Find me something to bang on," he told Dink. "Then get ready to move!"

"I'll keep an eye outside!" Ruth Rose said, heading for the garage door.

Dink glanced around the garage, then walked over to the tarp he'd hidden under. He yanked the tarp away and let out a low whistle. "Guys, look!"

Josh and Ruth Rose hurried over. Dink had uncovered four Happy Heart Dog Food boxes.

Dink tore open one flap and peeked inside.

"Just cans of dog food," he said.

"He must use the empty boxes to carry the fake money," said Ruth Rose.

Josh spotted an empty pail. "I bet I can get their attention with *this*!" he said.

Dink opened the window. Ruth Rose came over to stand beside him.

"Okay, Josh," Dink said. "Do it!"

Josh took a deep breath, then started pounding the bottom of the pail with the hammer.

The noise boomed through the garage like thunder.

"Now!" Josh said. He dropped the hammer and pail and bolted for the window.

The kids hopped out and crouched in the weeds.

A few seconds later, they heard the garage door creak open and Mr. Bent say, "Stay, Shorty!"

Then Dink heard Mrs. Bent say,

"Warden, someone's been in here. Something's written on the floor!"

That was all the kids needed to hear. They raced toward the trees on the other side of the house. In two minutes, they had crossed the high school playing field and were heading down Main Street.

"I sure hope Officer Fallon is in," Dink said, out of breath.

He was. The kids burst through his door with red faces.

Officer Fallon looked up. "What are you—"

"We found the counterfeiter!" all three kids yelled.

Chapter 11

Interrupting each other, the kids told Officer Fallon about the Bents.

Even before Officer Fallon heard about the Happy Heart Dog Food boxes, he was shouting orders into his telephone.

"Don't go back to Fox Lane!" were his last words before he leaped for the door and disappeared.

"Now what?" Dink asked.

"Why should we be left out?" Ruth

Rose asked. "Let's go watch!"

"Go where?" Josh asked. "He said to stay away—"

"Not Fox Lane," Dink interrupted. "The action is gonna be on Squall Island!"

Minutes later, they were catching their breath next to Officer Fallon's cruiser on River Road. The fog had lifted and they had a better view of Squall Island.

Dink peered across the river but saw only sand and rocks.

Out of breath, Josh sank to the ground. "I think I'm having a heart attack!" he moaned.

"Do you think Officer Fallon is out there?" Ruth Rose asked, squinting. "I don't see anyone."

The kids sat in the shade of the cruiser and watched the island.

Suddenly, Josh jumped to his feet.

"There they are!" he shouted.

Three figures had come around the island's other side. It was too far away to tell who they were, but Dink thought he could see Officer Fallon's dark uniform.

Then a fourth person came into view. He was pulling a small flat-bottomed boat behind him.

"It's Officer Fallon and Officer Keene!" Dink said. "They've got the Bents!"

The kids watched the group come closer. The water was nearly up to Officer Fallon's knees. He led the Bents, who were handcuffed. Officer Keene waded behind, pulling the boat. It was green!

"Look what's in the boat!" Josh said. "It's piled with money and dog food boxes!"

Nobody spoke as Officer Fallon led

the two counterfeiters to shore. The
Bents were wearing their long wading
boots. Their faces were angry as they
stumbled up the riverbank.

Officer Keene pulled the boat
ashore and loaded the counterfeit
money into the trunk of the cruiser.
Officer Fallon opened the rear door for
the Bents, then locked it once they were
inside.

"Good job," he said to the kids. He
looked at Josh. "Are your folks home?"

"I don't know," Josh answered.

"Meet me at your house in an hour," Officer Fallon said. Then he and Officer Keene hitched up their wet pants and climbed into the cruiser.

The car sped away, leaving the air filled with dust and pine needles.

"Why does Officer Fallon want to talk to your mom and dad?" Dink asked, grinning. "Are you in trouble?"

"Gee, I wonder what jail food is like!" Ruth Rose said.

Dink patted Josh's belly. "I heard they feed the prisoners worm waffles for breakfast!"

"Tee-hee," Josh said. "You guys are so funny! He probably wants to give me a reward for catching the Bents."

"You didn't catch them," Ruth Rose said. "The three of us did!"

"But we all know I'm the brains in this group," Josh said, smiling.

They cut through a field to get to Josh's house. Josh yanked open the back door and yelled, "Anybody home?"

No one answered. "Let's eat," Josh said. "I'll make some sandwiches."

They sat in Josh's backyard with jelly sandwiches, paper cups, and a container of milk.

"I wonder where the Bents made the money," Dink said. "Do you suppose they have a printing machine in that house?"

Josh put his sandwich down. "What would it be like to make money whenever you wanted?"

Dink heard a car roll into Josh's driveway. A door slammed and Officer Fallon came around the house.

"Can you spare some of that milk?" he asked Josh.

"Sure!" Josh filled a cup and handed it to Officer Fallon.

He took a long sip, then looked at the kids. "The Bents are locked up, but they're not talking. When they do, I expect we'll find out they were just the middle guys. Whoever is printing all those hundreds is still out there somewhere."

"But why did the Bents hide the money on Squall Island?" Josh asked.

"Easy to get to," Officer Fallon said. "With their boat at the bait shop, they could get out to the island in a few minutes."

"At first we thought they might be partners with Mr. Pinkowski," Dink said.

Officer Fallon nodded. "I can see why you thought so. I talked to Ron. He kept their boat in his yard. Then after Bent saw you kids on the island, he asked Ron to paint it. I guess he was afraid you would recognize it if you ever saw it again."

"Why did Mr. Pinkowski buy the calamine lotion?" Josh asked.

"Ron's a nice guy," Officer Fallon said. "I guess he noticed Bent was itching, so he bought him the lotion as a favor."

Officer Fallon glanced at Josh's barn. "Keep any animals in there?" he asked Josh.

"No," Josh said. "The twins and I want a pony, but Dad says they're too much work."

"How about a dog?" Officer Fallon said. "I just happen to have a nice friendly basset hound who needs a good home."

Josh's eyes lit up. "Really?"

Officer Fallon smiled. "Maybe you two should get to know each other."

He whistled. Around the corner jogged Officer Keene, leading a short-legged dog with droopy ears.

"It's Shorty!" Ruth Rose said.

"You kids already know this pooch?" Officer Fallon said.

"He was at the Bents' house," Dink explained. "He almost gave away our hiding place!"

Officer Fallon stroked the dog's velvety ears. "Well, his owners are going to prison for a long time. He needs a new home."

Josh kneeled down and patted the dog's silky coat.

"Hey, doggie," he said. "You wanna live here?"

The dog gave Josh a lick with his long pink tongue, then plopped to the ground and rolled over.

"He likes me!" Josh said.

"I was counting on it," Officer Fallon said. He dropped the leash into Josh's hand and headed for his car. "Have your folks call me!" he said as he left.

"Thanks, Officer Fallon!" Josh called.

"What should we name him?" Josh asked after a minute.

"He already has a name," Ruth Rose reminded Josh. "Shorty."

Josh shook his head. "That's a terrible name. If you were short, would you want to be called Shorty?"

"Josh is right," Dink said. "We can come up with a better name than that."

But when Josh's parents came home

an hour later, the kids still hadn't picked a name.

When Josh finally got permission to keep the dog, he still had no name.

Later that night, Dink, Josh, and Ruth Rose drifted off to sleep in their bedrooms.

The short-legged dog with droopy ears snored at the end of Josh's bed.

But he still had no name.

HAVE YOU READ ALL THE BOOKS IN THE

A TO Z MYSTERIES®

SERIES?

Help Dink, Josh, and Ruth Rose . . .

...solve mysteries from A to Z!

Collect clues with
Dink, Josh, and Ruth Rose
in their next exciting
adventure!

THE
JAGUAR'S
JEWEL

Dink ran his fingers over the striped wallpaper. Just above his head, he felt a thin crack. He followed the crack with his fingers until he felt another crack, this one running down toward the floor.

Dink jumped back as if his hand had been burned. "Guys!" he shouted.

Josh and Ruth Rose came running into James's office.

Dink showed them his discovery. "I think it's a secret door!" he said.